STARLIT SCARS

NAYSA BILLA

Made with ♥ on the Notion Press Platform
www.notionpress.com

Contents

Contents

Contents

Preface

As I embarked on my poetic journey, I never imagined anyone but me would witness my words. Yet, it is precisely this vulnerability that has allowed me to craft verses that are written with unflinching candor. The mosaic that these pieces put together create is an intimate reflection of a sensitive and introspective soul.

Despite the uniqueness of individual experiences, I believe all of us share a minute identical sensitivity that we often refuse to embrace.

As a poet I invite you to join me on this journey, to delve into the abyss of emotions that colour each of our minds and hearts in shades that elude our eyes.

May you find fragments of yourself engraved within the lines I've penned, inspired by the beauty and complexity of the human experience.

Starlit Scars

Crimson red that made me brave,
Escaping these torturous hours,
Screaming in the blinding pain
that followed these starlit scars.

Perhaps they gave me strength,
These starlit scars that shine,
Perhaps the mayhem of these bruises
is what makes my soul mine.

Wonders

*When your eyes close
and stars begin to show,
When you find fire in the rain
And warmth in the snow.*

*The colours that don't exist,
Dancing in your mind.
Euphoria in the sky,
One of a kind.*

*When a smile escapes your lips
and your eyes close to see
the wonders of the world
made just for thee.*

Near

The risks taken to have you by my side,
The things I'd wrestle for you,
I wonder what drives me
to do the things I do.

Maybe it's the adrenaline,
Maybe it's the fear,
Or maybe it's the peace
of having you near.

Stolen

Pining for stolen kisses,
Dreaming of alternate reality,
Finding our mesmer
Away from actuality.

In a utopian life,
Perhaps another day,
Until then I will settle
for these stolen moments away.

Apocalypse

Your hands over my heartbeat,
Your fingertips circling my skin;
Kiss me back to life
till I'm the most alive I've ever been.

Merciless passion,
Embracing my lips;
Your voice, whirling my thoughts,
Victim to an apocalypse.

Ink

The ink bleeds
and the pages turn,
Syllables flow in ached descriptions
of the love I've learnt.

My words are crimson
and my hands are bruised blue,
For even a million words
are far too few.

Morning

• 7 •

Petals like silk,
The sun in my face.
The raven that greets us
in these frosty days.

The eyes of the sky,
The peacock's might
but even on the romantic mornings,
I miss the night.

Loving Memory

Reminisce of those we had
and dreams of those we miss,
The ephemeral evocation and
nostalgia of their withering kiss.

In the loving memory of
everything we lost,
The days go by in their remembrance,
Within morning dew and winter frost.

Pianist

Grateful to your hands,
The blessed duty they served,
Telling a thousand stories,
Without uttering a single word.

The elegant fingers,
Their grasp on our minds
and the musicality they deliver,
One of a kind.

The pianist's beauty
is that he barely sees
how bewitched the listeners are,
Whose souls he touches with his keys.

Midnight Blue

When the universe sleeps
and awakens, eyes swell with rue,
Tears glittering like stars
in a sea of midnight blue.

Their passionate twinkling
and their soft cries.
Until the midnight blue
of the night dies.

Cracked Walls

When the world ends
fear would elude me
for your embrace is everything
heaven could be.

Blinding lights and cracked walls,
Your heart beating loud,
It would still taste like heaven
and champagne clouds.

All I could hope
is that you'll be by my side
for I'd like to be in heaven
when I watch the stars collide.

Memento Mori

They all say
"This intoxicating poison
It's effects, divine,
That warm my heart
and quiet my mind.

If it takes poison to heal,
If it eases the cry.
If death is what it takes,
Memento mori
(We must die)."

Bouquet

We close our eyes
and feel the universe's kiss
for only a deity
could create love like this.

The love I live for,
This love of ours;
It's like the sky gifted to me
a bouquet of stars.

Soon

Clocks can't fathom
the time I crave,
Martyrs would shy
from the risks I'd brave.

For the world could end
at the next first light
but for a minute with you,
There's no war I wouldn't fight.

I would bow to the sun,
Climb to the moon;
All if it would mean,
You wouldn't leave so soon.

Sun

Blessed be the sun that coaxes your mornings
and pardons your rest,
For I covet to be by your side forever
like the sun that christens your skin
but doesn't know it's worth the way I do.

See You Soon

*We change colour
like the morning skies;
We scream with pain
between goodbyes.*

*We covet our friends
who promised "See you soon."
So close yet so far
like our darling moon.*

Stardust

*Where we came from
is a mystery,
Where we'll go
is a thing of trust.
Enjoy this moment with me,
Fellow creature
birthed from stardust.*

Amber

We wonder if the brutal kindness
justify the pretty lies;
But I'd rather see deception
than tears in your amber eyes.

Wanderlust

In death, we reminisce
the intricacies of our lives.
We marvel at the spectacles
that precede our demise.

Before our fingers run cold
and our ashes turn to dust.
We remember the adventures
of our wanderlust.

Ash

Their skin turns grey as ash,
Those who shudder of cold,
Away from the silver towers
that embellish cities of gold.

Beneath the beauty,
Behind the facade, they hide;
Just like the moon,
The world has a dark side.

Downpour

Thunder grumbling,
Chill in the air,
Sun hidden beneath
the clouds, with care.

Lightning in the sky,
Parched earths quenched by rain,
Tears of the sky, falling on my skin,
Electric downpour keeping me sane.

Mockingbird

In a world of darkness,
You'd be the moon;
I can cry for melodies,
But you'd be the tune.

I might be a writer...
But you'll always be my words.
I sing to the echoes of your voice,
Like a yearning mockingbird.

Drug

Your spirit talking to mine,
Devotion, much as there could be.
If I'm drowning in passionate currents,
You'd be my sea.

If I were to sprout wings,
You'd be my loving sky;
You'd be the seductive drug
that gets me high.

Saturn

Just this once, time could stop
while our hearts would race
and we'd have a forever full of
magic and mystique to embrace.

Conundrums of our celestial neverland,
The blissful liberty to never return,
Whispers between yearning breaths,
"Life is better on Saturn."

Perfume

My mind gets clouded
and my soul starts to shine
with the rhythm of your pulse,
With your hands in mine.

My eyes are blessed,
My heart is gold,
My skin is electric,
My hands are cold.

When I hear your voice,
Blood red roses bloom
and chaos unleashes
when I smell perfume.

Kill Me First

When I feel your fingertips
dancing on my skin,
I see the beauty of fear
and the purity of sin.

When you hold me in your arms,
Suffocating me with your eyes,
The venerated crushing of my soul,
As if you're my adored demise.

When you break me with
unfathomable love, I foresee that
I will neither die of hunger nor of thirst;
We'll either die together
or your absence will kill me first.

Love, Love

There's fire in my spirit,
War in my heart,
Screams in my mind,
Pain in my art.

But regardless of the violence
that engulfs my soul,
When I love, I love,
I love complete, I love whole.

When I love, I love.
I love like the stars, the trees,
Like the moon, I love like wings
have set me free.

Rome

Bring the heavens for me to rest,
Carve out the intricacies of Rome
but I'll still crawl into your heart
and call it home.

Universe

The nostalgia of a universe
where we belong,
The universe of arresting delirium
and hypnosis to nightingales' song.

The world you created
with bare hands and heart;
The world of incandescent souls,
Embellished apart.

Melodies getting louder,
Hearts beating fast,
Time should collapse
for this universe to last.

Homesick

The incurable longing
to live on the moon
while I'm fastened to foreign ground,
Rebellious thoughts encircling Neptune.

The incorrigible heat up close
but the ethereal tranquillity from afar,
This uncanny resemblance
makes me homesick for stars.

Desires

Yearning to be cherished,
Devoted to a sin,
Too much love to offer;
Love that kills her from within.

She will climb to the heavens
to bring you peace;
Too much love to offer,
Too much she'd do to appease.

"Will you die for me?"
She'd throw herself into fires,
Marvelled at what it is to be loved,
But she is the love she desires.

Friends

Drowning in your words,
Left with no choice,
Succumbed to the poison,
Your catastrophic voice.

The venom will attack my mind
and pain me into being mesmerised
and pollute my lungs
and leave me paralysed.

And I know I'll be hurt beyond repair
by the time it ends
but there's nothing more romantic
than dying with your friends.

Fire

There's silence in his voice
and noise in his mind.
I'm the music he craves
and the tranquillity he'll find.

There's hurt in my blood,
He's the solace I desire.
I shiver from the cold
and he is the fire.

Friendship

She heard his voice
and found home in its cracks
and he held her bleeding skin
like it's everything he lacks.

He fell for her mind,
She fell for his heart;
They fell into friendship,
A fanatical start.

Heard her through the eyes,
One of a kind.
The skin he once
stopped from bleeding,
Love, redefined.

Strangers

Addicted to the melody
of his pretty lies.
To learn a new language
is reading a stranger's eyes.

Electricity pulsating through my veins
under a stranger's fingertips,
Dancing to the symphony of his voice,
Yearning kisses to a stranger's lips.

The touch of a stranger,
His breath on my skin.
A stranger's ephemeral love
that ends in a whirlwind.

Like Me

I cherish it when you were cruel
and I worship you when you're kind.
In mesmer of the touch that you planted
and the garden you left behind.

What's the magic in your breath
that filled my lungs with air?
How do your graceful fingers
heal my wounds with care?

The lunacy of your voice,
Your deranged eyes that set me free,
Make me question,
Are you insane like me?

Promise

The promise of tomorrow,
The hopes of a next midnight,
Falser than vows made in wine; yet,
Purer than promises made under moonlight.

These frenzies might end far too soon,
Weights on our chest would be lighter,
Touches to the skin would spark whimsy,
Starlight would feel brighter.

The promise of tomorrow,
The hopes of the next morning sun,
Falser than a harmless ocean,
Yet purer than your dreams with "the one".

Worth

I'll swim through oceans,
Fight a thousand battles with fate;
I'll give you the air from my lungs
All if you promise to be worth the wait.

I'll burn like the sun,
Let you drive me insane,
I'll tear my heart out of my chest,
All if you promise to be worth the pain.

Fall Out

Memories will fade,
Our minds are such,
Our ashen skin
will forget each pining touch.

We will grow weary of loss
and our hearts will go cold
but nothing can kill
a yearning soul.

We will fall into the flames of hell
or rise towards heaven above
but the tortured soul of man
can never fall out of love.

Mayhem

Your perfume blooming in my lungs,
The ocean of your eyes pulsating in my veins;
I've become the sound of your music,
Crystals that pour when you cherish the rain.

I built a home within the cracks of your voice,
I'm coloured with darkness that echoes in your mind;
I am a mayhem of all I admire,
A labyrinth of the world your words leave behind.

If I am everyone I've ever loved
and everything I've ever seen,
I have eyes for you alone
so it's only you I've ever been.

Worth the Broken Heart

Graceful kisses down my neck,
My hand touching his,
A thousand tokens of love,
A million moments to miss.

My hands through his hair,
His voice dancing in my ears;
He promised me nothing
but my biggest fears.

For I know love is falser
than vows made in wine
but each second with you is worth
the broken heart you'll leave behind.

Empath

I'll hold your broken heart together,
Do whatever you please,
Mend your aching soul,
Put your mind to ease.

Someday you'll ask,
"Why do this for me?"
You wouldn't understand but
to care, comes effortlessly.

I'll give you the sun,
Wipe the tears in your eyes,
Colour your life in hints of red,
Between greys and black skies.

Sin

Magic in his hands,
Fingertips gracing my skin,
His lips touching mine,
The most alive I've ever been.

Apocalyptic smile, abyssal eyes,
An ocean to drown in.
Oxygen leaving my lungs,
To covet is wrong and I'm devoted to sin.

She Fell Harder

He fell first, she fell harder,
Mystical enigma love is,
He caressed her bare skin with pride,
She cherished each secretly imperious kiss.

He fell first, she fell harder,
His eyes glinting with glee,
She was blinded in his abyssal affection,
Drowning in its suffocating sea.

He fell first, she fell harder
She fell hard, from the sky,
He embellished his words in love
and she believed each glittering lie.

Lost His Mind

She said in love he loses his mind,
Musical screaming and passionate fights,
Trinkets of forgiveness and tears of guilt,
The fire is not nearly as painful as it is bright.

Undying adoration sparking between the two,
"What an enigma this love is,"
She said, reminiscing his devoted kind eyes,
"He even slapped me and it felt like a kiss."

I Dare You

Affection burning in my blood,
The musicality of your beating heart;
I worship you like a deity,
Admire your skin like art.

I will be your eyes in the darkness,
Your wings as you wish to flee,
With enigmatic compassion I'm everything you desire,

I dare you now, to not fall in love with me.

Regardless

She fell in love with his tortured soul,
Adores his eyes that sparkle like stars.
Cherishes each fleeting touch of his sun-kissed skin,
She fell in love with even his scars.

In this promise of love and obsessive passion,
She mend his bruises while her's brutally burn
She loves him regardless,
Brings him whatever his heart yearns.

"Do you promise to love me, as I do you?"
She asked with hope glimmering in her eyes,
"But darling, you love me regardless" he said,
"For that is where your loyalty lies."

Shameless

• 48 •

Much too soon, it gets dark,
An abyss with nothing in sight
but the stars burn shamelessly;
The stars burn bright.

Bleeding

We saw her last with a bleeding smile,
Bleeding ears and bleeding eyes,
Bleeding heart, with few beats left
Bleeding face buried within muffled cries.

Chest tightened, hands gone cold,
Bleeding heart started beating fast;
Though there was not much left to say,
Bleeding throat, screamed at last.

The screams consoling her bleeding mind,
As her bleeding body started withering away
but the blood stains, of the bleeding girl,
Those, forever, shall stay.

Pretty Girl

These cigarettes he lights
on these walks that we take,
Smoke that leaves his strawberry lips
and the hearts that they break.

He's got wings to fly, eyes that sparkle
with tears of pearl,
He's got the chest of a god, arms of a deity
and she was just a pretty girl.

Wrong Time

*We kissed each other in the promise
of forgetting that night,
Of not wanting each other too much
until the time was right.*

*Laced with love, with a glimpse of fear,
The night saw real kisses,
Hopeful yet hollow, harmonic with hysteria,
Ended in fake promises.*

*Maybe we could work, in a different world,
In a different song, with a different rhyme,
I'll let the futile faith triumph
or I'll recite this tale, right person wrong time.*

Chokehold

My breath, at your mercy,
Your fingers, gracing my neck,
Hold me together, if you please
or leave me a wreck.

I will fall on my knees,
Kiss at your feet;
Your control is comforting,
The captivity bittersweet.

Play me like a violin,
Let me be the muse to your dreadfully gorgeous eyes.
Mould me into someone you can love,
I'm yours, you've got me hypnotised.

Lovers

Lovers falling in love,
while they're waiting for their turn,
Blissfully unaware that it's each other
that their hearts yearn for.

Lovers falling in love
but they're too scared to fall,
Quiet in their admiration,
Pretending they can't love at all.

Lovers falling in love
while they are sinking in burning desire,
Scared to fall to their fates with each other
because they fear that fire with fire will make a bigger fire.

Paper Things

Admiring these stolen rings,
These delicate paper things,

These cigarettes that burn too fast,
while we stare at the vividly grey skies,
the way this time flies.

Fire

It isn't hell if she likes the way it burns,
They are the thunder that strikes the rain,
Drove to madness, chasing oblivion,
Becoming insane.

The euphony in the rage,
It tears her apart,
The scars that are left behind
heal her soul yet break her heart.

But she let it hurt,
Let herself burn in desire.
What is love, if it isn't torturously beautiful?
What is love if not fire?

Almost Asleep

Hearts beat faster,
For a second you stop to feel,
The musicality of the wind
starts to become surreal.

Skies seem clear,
Stars burn brighter above;
Maybe I've lost my mind
or maybe we're delusional in love.

Laughs

Tears keep streaming from hearts that hurt
but ours don't trickle at all;
Lovers keep falling in love
but we're too scared to fall.

Dreamers keep dreaming
but dreams are for the cloying few,
Tears should keep streaming, but
you'd be surprised what we laugh through.

His Eyes

Her mind was ordinary,
Not really obscene;
Her beauty was neither mighty
nor serene.

It was his vibrant eyes that
coloured her in pink and blue;
It was his eyes that
saw so much within so few.

Blessed, those eyes,
Mesmerised with all they saw;
The way those eyes
torturously adored each flaw.

The eyes that saw her in the
monotonous sea of greys and blacks,
Blessed, those eyes,
Painted hints of red between her white lies.

Part Hell

An oceanic abyss
within her brown eyes,
She's friends with the wind,
Her spirit startles the skies.

But there's hidden scars that haunt her,
Demons she's had to fight,
That stole her slumber,
So many nights.

She wore beauty and darkness,
Both equally well.
She's always been part goddess
and she'll always be part hell.

Silver Tears

The sunshine glistening,
Except here they shudder of cold.
The gilded prisons
where tears in silver fall on cheeks of gold.

Where smiles are scarce
and words are cruel;
Where the lands are serene,
Every man bears priceless jewels.

Adorned with diamonds
yet embellished with lies;
Their loveless bleak reality
is one hidden with glorified trinkets
and that's their beautiful brutality.